I0880519

OUTDOOR LIVING™

BIKE TREKKING

MELODY WAYNE AND CHRIS HAYHURST

ROSEN PUBLISHING
NEW YORK

Published in 2016 by The Rosen Publishing Group, Inc.
29 East 21st Street, New York, NY 10010

Copyright © 2016 by The Rosen Publishing Group, Inc.

First Edition

All rights reserved. No part of this book may be reproduced in any form without permission in writing from the publisher, except by a reviewer.

Library of Congress Cataloging-in-Publication Data

Wayne, Melody.
Bike trekking / Melody Wayne and Chris Hayhurst.—First Edition.
pages cm.— (Outdoor living)
Includes index.
Audience: Grades: 7–12.
ISBN 978-1-4994-6235-7 (Library bound)
1. Cycling—Juvenile literature. 2. Bicycle touring—Juvenile literature. I. Hayhurst, Chris. II. Title.
GV1043.7.W39 2016
796.6'2—dc23

Manufactured in China

CONTENTS

INTRODUCTION

The thrill of riding a bike on your own for the first time is an amazing experience. The freedom to go fast, to go further than you could before in a shorter time, into different places in the city, or to zoom along country trails feels wonderful. But more than just a recreational vehicle, bikes can also help you to discover places in a way that you may not have considered before. Imagine seeing the world while pedaling through it on a bike. You get to go fast and far, but still be up close and personal to all the things that you would not be able to touch from a car,

Bike trekking is great exercise for people who like being outdoors, but you must be prepared for weather conditions and bring supplies for a long ride.

or from high up in an airplane or a helicopter. Bikes allow us to be close to the ground, to feel the dirt beneath our feet and see the sights up close. Faster than walking, but more hands-on than driving, bike trekking allows you to see the world in a totally different way. Best of all, you're on your own steam, not polluting the air in a gas-powered vehicle, and you can stop and go, slow down, or speed up as you please.

Of course, bike trekking, which we'll be talking about in depth in this resource, is more than just hopping on any bike and taking off. It's important to know what kind of condition you the rider need to be in, what kind of bike you will need (because not all bikes are built for all terrains), and what kind of other equipment you might need besides a bike and a helmet. You need to learn the basics of keeping your bide in good working condition. You also need to understand how to fix your bike properly because a flat tire or a broken chain can be the end of your trekking adventure. Bike trekking also isn't a leisure activity. It's a sport, and it can be a dangerous one at that. It may be incredibly exciting and rewarding, but you have to know the rules of the road.

So before you head off on your next bike trekking adventure, this resource can help you to learn what bike trekking is all about, how to condition your body, and how to care for your equipment. By the end, you'll be ready to explore the world.

CHAPTER 1

PLAN OUT YOUR TREK

The first thing you need to understand about bike trekking is that it is a physical outdoor sport that can take you away from home for days on end. Those who don't like bad weather, sweaty days, going off road, or sleeping in a tent need not attempt this sport. It is a major challenge both physically and mentally. Before you run out and buy all the gear: a bike, panniers, tools, and camping equipment, take a step back and make sure that this is for you. If you've never tried camping, it might be worth it just to do a weekend camping trip just to make sure you're up for everything involved in bike trekking.

If you already have a bike, you are well on your way to getting started. Just about any bike will do as long as it is strong, tuned up, and fits you. If you don't have a bike, you should be able to pick up a used one through the want ads or the Internet, or you can find a new or gently used one at your local bike store. The salespeople

The most important piece of equipment on a trek is the bike. Make sure to get information about different types of bikes so that you select the best one for your needs.

at bike stores can usually help you find exactly what bike will fit you and your needs best.

Once you have a bike, it is time to look into the rest of the gear. Again, shop around. Buying used equipment is often a smart move, especially if you're not 100 percent sure trekking is for you. If you have a friend who has been trekking before, ask him or her question you have about gear. A friend's input on what works best can save you a lot of time and money.

OK. You've got the gear and the desire. Are you ready to ride? Are you in shape? Can you handle all the miles of pedaling up and down hills with a loaded bike? A good way to answer these questions is by going on a few short practice rides. If you're planning to go on a long trip in a month or two, get out and do several shorter day trips first. Load up your panniers with the things that you will bring on your extended trip and get a feel for what it is like to pedal all day long weighted down with gear. You can learn a lot on short rides like these.

If you don't have a lot of time before your first multiday trek, never fear. On long trips—those of at least a week—you'll get in shape naturally as you go. The first few days may seem difficult, but eventually your leg muscles will get used to the work and the miles will become easier.

The most important thing to realize about getting started in bicycle trekking—or any sport for that matter—is that you will get better over time. As life on the bike becomes more familiar, it also

Longer bike trekking trips may require using camping skills. You should also be prepared to carry a lot of equipment.

gets easier. No one is born an expert in anything, so just get out there and have fun!

DIFFERENT WAYS TO TREK

There are many different ways to trek by bicycle. In fact, you could say that every person treks in his or her own way—in his or her own direction and pace, and with individual ideas of what to see and do.

SIGHTSEEING TREKS

Although most bike trekking involves long rides, and serious bike trekkers carry their own bikes and equipment, it is possible to take a short trek, even if you are visiting a city, and even if you didn't bring a bike. Some cities have begun bike sharing programs. It is part of an effort to reduce pollution from cars and to reduce street traffic, but some tourists are using city bike sharing programs as a way to trek through unfamiliar cities and see the sights. The bikes are usually set up at stations around a city. Anyone can rent a bike, usually with a credit card, and then he or she has it for a certain period of time. Bikes can also be dropped off at another station. That way, a tourist can ride around the city, hopping on and off rented bikes, and see all the sights on his or her very own bike trekking tour!

For example, you might want to ride your bike between the furthest points on the map of America, from Anchorage, Alaska, to Miami, Florida. Or perhaps you want to ride across the country, from Portland, Maine, to San Diego, California. Some trekkers may want a shorter trip, like across their home state, or just across the county. There are other kinds of treks that might take you to places outside of the country that are unfamiliar, like doing a tour down Mexico's Baja Peninsula or a journey around the world.

Where you want to ride often determines the type or style of bicycle trekking required to get there. Trek across the remote desert outback of Australia, for instance, and you will probably need a support van to carry your food and water. Ride 100 miles (160 kilometers) from your house to the beach and back, and you can probably carry everything you need for the two- or three-day trip.

Something else you need to consider is your physical ability. Are you fit? How much experience do you have riding for long periods and over different terrain? If you are in great shape, you probably won't need a sag wagon—a car or van that rides along to provide support—and you shouldn't have any trouble carrying all your gear yourself. Likewise, if you are an experienced camper, pitching a tent may seem more inviting than spending a night in a hostel or motel room. But if you have never been on a trek before and can't set up a campsite to save your life, you may be better off making your first journey with a group under the leadership of a professional guide who can teach you all the necessary skillsflash and help you if there is a problem along the way. If you have no experience at all, it is unwise to set out on a solo journey around the globe, or even across the county.

A self-contained bike tour is one in which the riders carry everything they need to get from start to finish. They stuff sleeping bags and tents into their panniers; have flashlights, maps, and compasses or GPS systems within reach; and pack enough food and water to ensure that they will be well-nourished and hydrated throughout the trip. A fully supported trip, in the other hand, is one in which the riders carry nothing but themselves on their bikes. A sag wagon, carrying everyone's gear, accompanies the riders from place to place. Many trips fall between these two extremes, with riders using a support vehicle for some of the distance or stopping at motel rooms instead of backcountry campsites.

Sag wagons carry most of the equipment, which lightens a bike trekker's load, but it requires coordinating stops and sticking to a schedule.

Coordinating with other riders means pre-planning your route, scheduling breaks, and sticking to a plan.

Another decision bike trekkers must make is whether to ride off-road or on-road. Some bikers prefer to ride through country trails instead of paved roads and highways. Others would rather stick to the roads, where the riding is smooth and fast, and where help, if it is needed, is only a car away, and often there is both GPS and phone signal in case of emergency. Trails usually require a

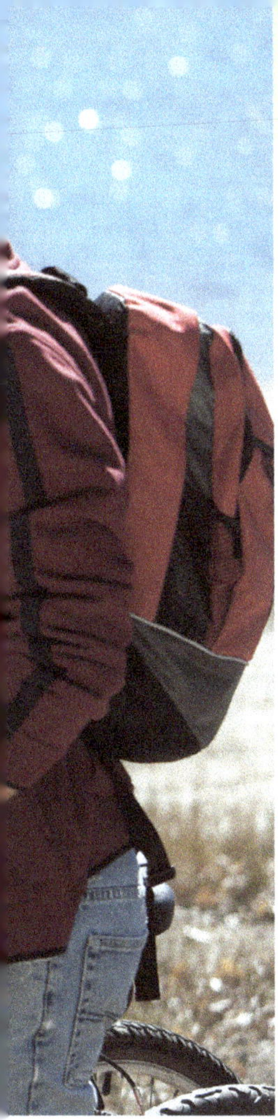

mountain bike, whereas maintained highways are sometimes better traveled on a road bike.

Regardless of what kind of bicycle trekking you want to do, you need to plan your trip well. Think about the terrain you will be riding on. What kind of bike does that require? Remember that you won't be able to switch bikes mid-trek. You also need to think about where you will sleep at night if the trek will go overnight. If you're not used to camping in a tent, you need to check to see whether there are other accommodations close to where you will be stopping for the night. If not, you may have to coordinate stopping, or starting the next morning with your group, if you are going with other people. You also need to think about the meals you will have. If you are packing everything and camping, then whatever food you have needs to last you through the trek. Once you consider all of these different things and plan them out properly, all you need to do is get on the bike for a nice ride.

CHAPTER 2

WHAT YOU WILL NEED

Once you have a plan about where you would like to go, how long it will take you to get there and back, and what kind of terrain you will be riding on along the way, it's time to start thinking about what you need to take with you on the trip. Consider where you are going to stop. Will you need camping equipment? Food and water? What will the weather be like? What kind of protective clothing do you need to have? These things will determine what you have to carry. The next thing you need to do is figure out how to get all of those things onto your bike, since that is the main piece of equipment you will need. The bike is your vehicle, your home, and your suitcase rolled into one.

Good touring bikes take many shapes and sizes, but all have one thing in common: durability. They have to be strong. Today, many cyclists use mountain bikes which have fat wheels, beefy frames, and a compact size. They can handle a variety of different riding conditions—from trails to rugged dirt roads to paved highways. Others swear by the classic touring bike, which has a larger frame, fenders, and dropped handlebars. Whether you choose to ride a mountain bike, a road bike, or one that's somewhere in between is up to you and what kind of conditions you expect on your trek.

WHAT YOU NEED TO KNOW ABOUT BIKES

Bikes are complicated pieces of machinery. To have fun and stay safe while bike trekking, you need to have at least a minimum understanding of how your bicycle works. Here's a list of things you may find on your bike:

Bottom bracket: This is where your cranks are attached to the bike. The cranks are enabled to spin thanks to the bottom-bracket bearing, which is held in the bottom-bracket shell.

Brakes: Well, you do need to slow down once in a while.

Chain-rings: The three cogs, smallest on the inside and largest on the outside, fitted to the chain set. The chain fits over a chain-ring's teeth.

Chain set: The complete set of crank, chain-rings, and bottom bracket.

Chain stay: The two bottom frame tubes that run from the bottom-bracket shell to the hub of the rear wheel.

Cranks: The two metal arms on either side of the bike that run from the pedals to the bottom-bracket axle.

It's important to understand all the equipment needed for a successful bike trekking trip. You have to know how your bike works and how to use the supplies you will need.

Derailleurs: There are two: front and rear. They move the chain when you shift gears.

Fork: The fork holds the front wheel and houses the steerer tube.

Freewheel: This allows the rear wheel to keep rolling when you stop pedaling.

Handlebars: These are used to steer the bike. This is where your grips and brake levers are mounted. If you have a mountain bike, your shifters will be up there, too.

Headset: This houses the bearings that allow the steerer tube to rotate. It is located right above the top front point of the frame.

Hub: There are two hubs, one at the center of each wheel. They support the spokes and hold the ball bearings that enable the wheels to spin smoothly.

Pedals: Most pedals are now clipless, meaning there are no straps, just metal cleats to which your shoes attach.

Presta/Schrader valves: Your bike tires will use one of these valves to maintain air pressure. The Presta valve is thinner and used in most mountain bikes. The Schrader is larger and also used in car tires, which means you can pump air into your tires at a gas station. Make sure you have a pump that fits your valve.

Quick releases: These devices allow you to quickly tighten or loosen your seat post and wheels.

Rims: The two metal hoops on which the tubes and tires are mounted.

Saddle: The bike seat.

Seat post: The tube to which the seat is attached.

Shifters: Mechanisms mounted on the handlebars or on the bike frame that allow you to change gears.

Spokes: Thin metal cables that connect a wheel's hub to the rim.

Top tube: The horizontal top part of the frame that runs from the headset to the seat post.

Most of what the bike trekker carries is packed into sturdy bags called panniers. Panniers attach to metal racks that are fastened to the bike's frame. If you find that your panniers just aren't big enough to hold everything you need, you can strap your extra stuff to the rear rack, which sits conveniently right behind the bike seat, over the rear wheel. Finally, you can mount a small bag on your handle-bars and fill it with items you may need on the road, like your sunglasses, maps, a phone with GPS, and money. If you pack for an extended, self-contained trip, one where it is just you the road and your gear, your rig may end up looking more like a tank than a bike.

How you pack your bike depends on how long you plan to ride, whether there will be towns every few miles or only every few days, and where you plan to stay. It also depends on the weather—if you ride in the winter in New England, for instance, you will need to carry supplies to brave the cold.

If you will be camping along your route, you need to pack the appropriate camping gear. Make sure you divide the big things—like the tent, stove, and cook set—among all the riders in your group.

For longer bike trekking trips that require camping, make a checklist of all the supplies in your pack so that you don't leave anything behind on any part of the trip.

That way one person won't be stuck carrying all of the weight. If you ride alone, you had better pack light or else you need to be really strong.

If you will be staying in youth hostels or other accommodations that provide a kitchen and a place to sleep, your load will be much lighter. But remember you have to plan out these stops in advance. Likewise, if there are many towns along your route, you can generally carry less food and stop at local stores to pick up whatever you need along the way.

The key to an enjoyable trek is packing everything you need while paying attention to the details, like weight. Consider what items are essential and what things you can do without. For example, a stove may be unnecessary if you are staying at hostels, or if there are many towns along the way where you can cook or purchase prepared food. Making good decisions while you are packing can mean that a very steep hill at the end of the day is easier to mount.

WHAT EQUIPMENT TO BRING

Some items should be essential for any long bike trek. Things that will keep you safe, fed, and healthy, and your bike in good working condition are all essentials. You will also need to pack whatever toiletries you regularly use, such as your toothbrush and toothpaste. And don't forget the little extras—things that might take up space but that will keep you entertained, like a book, camera, journal, or playing cards.

ESSENTIAL EQUIPMENT

- Bungee cords
- Extra straps
- First-aid kit
- Handlebar bag
- Lights and reflectors for riding at night
- Maps or GPS
- Phone and battery charger
- Money
- Panniers (front and rear)
- Plastic bags
- Pocketknife
- Sunscreen
- Tool kit
- Water bottles
- Water purification system
- Pump (for tires)
- Cookstove
- Cooking set (pan, pot, bowl, mug, utensils)
- Flashlight
- Fuel bottle/extra fuel
- Ground cloth
- Matches/lighter
- Pack towel (chamois)
- Sleeping bag
- Sleeping pad
- Tent

WHAT TO WEAR

Try to keep in mind that the best clothes to take on your trek are light, easy to wash, and fast-drying. Some fabrics are also better choices than others. You may want to look into high-performance fabric clothing that athletes use as they will be fast-drying, will wick away sweat, and also usually have antimicrobial properties, which

Fabrics are now being made specifically for sports like bike trekking. Be sure to get clothing items that suit the weather, terrain, and length of the journey.

prevent odor. If you decide not to wear specialty fabrics, consider that not all fabrics are great for long treks.

Cotton may be comfortable when it is dry, but when it is wet, the fabric can be downright dangerous. Cotton absorbs moisture like sweat or rain, and holds it against your body. Wet clothes plus a cool breeze will make you feel much colder and could lead to hypothermia, a potentially life-threatening condition in which your body temperature drops to an unsafe level. Natural fibers may not make the best fabric choices for trekking. Instead look for synthetics such as polypropylene or fleece. These fabrics wick sweat from your skin so that they don't cool you down.

ESSENTIAL CLOTHING

- Bandanna
- Baseball cap
- Casual clothes
- Cycling gloves (to protect your hands and prevent blisters)
- Cycling shoes
- Cycling shorts (the padding prevents saddle sores and chafing)
- Cycling socks (two pairs)
- Cycling tights
- Fleece and polypropylene top and bottom
- Fleece hat
- Fleece sweater
- Helmet
- Long-sleeve polypropylene top
- Sandals or running shoes
- Shorts
- Short-sleeve polypropylene jersey (preferably with pockets)
- Sunglasses
- Swimsuit
- Underwear
- Waterproof jacket and pants

TREKKING TOOLS

There are few components on your bike more important than your pedals. Although most pedals pretty much look the same, the fact is there are many different kinds. The biggest difference between pedals is how they fasten to your feet.

Being able to use tools to repair a bike will prevent any lengthy delays on your bike trek.

Some pedals come with straps and plastic or metal toe cups. You place your foot on the pedal, snug your toes into the toe cup, and cinch down the straps until your foot is held tightly in place. By securing your foot to the pedal, you can pull up as well as push down with every stroke.

Other pedals are called clipless (even though you do clip in to them) and eliminate the need for straps. Like ski bindings, they allow you to attach the sole of your shoe directly to a metal mechanism on the pedal. With a mere twist of your foot, you can clip in or out with ease. These pedals also allow you to push and pull, and

ESSENTIAL TOOLS

- Adjustable wrench
- Allen keys
- Chain tool
- Crank-arm wrench (to fit your crank)
- Crescent wrench
- Extra nuts and bolts
- Freewheel tool
- Liquid lubricant
- Patch kit
- Pedal wrench
- Pliers
- Pump
- Screwdrivers (flat and Phillips head)
- Spare chain links
- Spare spokes
- Spare tire
- Spare tube
- Spoke wrench
- Tire irons

are very popular among serious cyclists.

So which style is right for you? You'll need to try both types of pedals to see which one works best for your style of riding and which feels good to you.

It helps to be a mechanic when you go on extended touring trips. Your bike can break down anywhere—and will usually do so a long way from the nearest bike shop. Pack the bike tools and spare parts listed above every time you go on a ride and you'll be able to work your way out of almost any problem short of a broken frame. Just make sure you know how to use everything before you go!

CHAPTER 3

BE PREPARED

While it's a good idea to be in decent physical shape before you go off on a bike trek, it isn't really a requirement. One of the nice things about doing this kind of activity is that it can be a means to getting in shape. The only thing you really need is the ability to ride a bike and a desire to see the world at your own pace. However, it is important that you have the basics of being able to take care of your own health and know how to fix your bike. In the last section, the essential tools, equipment, and gear were outlined. Now you need some basics in how to use all of these items.

You never know when your bike might break down, and you may not be near a bike shop when it happens. If your chain breaks, you need to know how to fix it. You also need to have a basic understanding of first aid in case of minor injuries. On a long bike trek, it's not uncommon to fall and end up with a few scrapes and bruises. A good first-aid kit and know-how can keep you healthy.

When accidents happen, be prepared with a fist-aid kit to prevent injuries from becoming worse.

It also helps to have some camping skills, especially if you are going to be camping for an extended period. If you have camped before, camping with a bike is very similar to camping out of a backpack. The only real difference is how the equipment is transported. You carry everything you need with you. What's essential is that you know how to set up your tent, operate the cookstove, and keep an orderly camp. If you are cycling and a sudden storm hits, you will be glad you have your camping skills to help you weather the storm.

As you ride, the main thing you need to consider is how to save energy. This means finding a pace that you and your riding partners are comfortable with and taking regular breaks for food and water. In any group, some riders will be stronger than others. Ride at a pace you can all enjoy.

You can also conserve energy by learning how to pedal efficiently. Good pedaling technique—the kind of pedaling that lets you continue at the same pace for hours—comes with lots of practice. When you know how to "spin" your wheels, or pedal in circles by both pulling up and pushing down with each crank revolution, you will find that the hills become a lot easier and the flats a lot faster. In the end you will cover many more miles while expending much less energy.

An entire book could be written about how to draft, how to distribute the weight of your gear on your bike, how to get in touring shape, and how to climb, descend, and ultimately conquer the road. But the one thing most people never consider is motivation. If you're having trouble staying motivated during your tour, the days will seem endless and your body will become ragged. Always keep your goals in sight. If you know why you are on a tour in the first place and think it feels good to work your legs day in and day out, you will never get bored and you will find new things to keep you going each and every mile.

PREPPING YOUR BRAKES

Speeding down a hill with a fully loaded bike is exhilarating, but things can get down-right scary if your brakes don't work right. Check to make sure that your brakes are in order every time you board your bike. If they are not in the best shape, you need to try these methods to get them back in good working condition.

- Clean the wheel rims with rubbing alcohol and steel wool.
- Rub the brake pads with sandpaper. This should add texture to the pads, and better texture means better gripping power.
- Check to see if your brake pads are centered and aligned with

NEW EQUIPMENT

Being prepared also means learning about new technology that could make your ride more safe or efficient. Years ago, riders had to take maps. While these are still good and very useful, a GPS system on a phone can be even more helpful with added information about nearby places that can be found with only a click. There is also new equipment for riders being made all the time. A new type of bike helmet works like an airbag, popping up only when the rider is dislodged from the bike and risks falling, or hitting an object. The helmet, designed by two women in Sweden, fits around the neck of the rider and is "invisible" until needed. So far, it has not passed US bike helmet standards testing. Since 1999, bike helmets sold in the United States have to be strong enough to satisfy the Consumer Product Safety Commission (CPSC). Helmets sold in the US have brain buckets with the CPSC stamp of approval. Some helmets also have Snell certification as well. These helmets are considered to be the toughest in the world. Riders need to be aware of changing technology.

your wheel rims. Adjust if necessary.

- Take your bike into a shop for a tune-up.

FIXING A FLAT

Bikes sometimes get a flat tire, especially on rough terrain. It's important that all riders know how to fix one.

1. Pop the wheel off the bike.
2. Pull the tire off the rim with tire irons. This can be tricky. Slide a tire iron under the lip of the tire and pry the tire's edges over the rim. Take another tire iron and do the same thing a few inches farther down the rim. Soon you'll be able to slide the tire off the rim with your fingers or with a third tire iron.
3. Pull out the popped tube and either patch the hole or get a new tube.
4. Inspect the inside of the tire for anything sharp that might pop your new tube.
5. Pump some air into the new or repaired tube and place it on the rim beneath the lifted tire. Make sure the valve goes through the hole in the rim, and be careful not to punch or bunch up the tube.
6. Using your fingers, push the edge of the tire back under the lip of the rim.
7. Pump up the tire, put the wheel back on your bike, and you are ready to go.

FIXING THE WHEELS

One thing every bike trekker needs to know is how to remove a bike's wheels. If you get a flat, the wheel has to come off. If you need to squeeze your bike into a car, you may have to remove a wheel to make it fit. Want to lock your front and rear wheels together so a thief won't be tempted to steal them? You're going to have to take off a wheel first.

If you have a bike with quick-release wheels, the process of removing them is simple. You just need to flick open the release lever, detach the brake cable from the brake where the cable meets

Riders need to be prepared to change a flat tire to prevent delays and to make sure they can get safely to the next stop.

the brake right above the wheel, and pull the wheel out of the fork. Sometimes it's easier to get the wheels off if you turn your bike upside down.

The rear wheel is a little harder to get off than the front because you have to take the chain off first. To make it easier, just shift the chain so that it is all the way down in the lowest gear. After you undo the brake cable and the quick release, just twist and pull the wheel until it pops free of the chain.

TAKING CARE OF MEALS

If you are planning a self-contained biking trip but have no idea what to eat or how to cook it, don't worry. Cooking on the road is not that hard. With a few essential camp-kitchen appliances, a quick lesson in technique, and a shopping list, you'll be well on your way to becoming a great roadside cook. Here's what you need.

STOVE

A lightweight, compact stove will help you cook anything efficiently. Look for one with an adjustable flame that uses white gas. The salesperson at your local outdoors or camping store should be able to find one for you that is light and compact enough for a bike trek.

WATER

It's important to have fresh clean water to drink and cook with. To kill any dangerous microscopic creatures that may lurk in found water from rivers or lakes, you need to boil and filter the water, or treat it with iodine. Filters and iodine can also be found at outdoors or camping stores.

COOKING TOOLS

Good cookware for bike trekking is lightweight, easy to clean, and very compact. Look for a set that includes a pot, a pan, a cup, and a handle for gripping when pans get hot. Remember to bring utensils (fork, spoon, and a Swiss Army–style knife), a lighter, and a scouring pad for cleaning.

Longer bike treks may also require you to cook food. Think about this as you make the checklist for packing equipment.

This handy chart explains how much water you need on a regular day. Think about how much more you need after long, strenuous exercise like bike trekking.

HOW TO PACK FOOD

Packing is tricky. Take packaged foods out of their boxes or bags and repack in tight plastic bags so your food won't spill in your panniers. Don't bring canned or bottled foods because they are too bulky and heavy.

Don't stash dried fruit at the bottom of your pannier if you are going to want to snack on it all day as you ride. Likewise, don't put dinner food near the top of your bag because you won't need it until everything is unpacked anyway. Place each meal in a separate bag to make things easy to find and to minimize sorting when it's time to cook.

Make sure anything that might spill is double-bagged and placed near the bottom of your pannier. Liquids like cooking oil should be bottled in screw-top plastic containers.

CAMPING ETIQUETTE

Always cook, camp, and clean at least two hundred feet (sixty-one meters) away from any water source. Never leave food scraps lying around camp, as they will not only attract animals but will ruin the site for the next camper. The best way to make cleanup easy is by eating everything you cook—no leftovers.

SHOPPING

Food should be lightweight, come with minimal or no packaging, and be quick and easy to cook. Test-cook anything that you are not sure about before hitting the road. Here are some ideas:

Breakfast: Try quick-cooking oats, cereal, granola, bagels, and dried fruit such as apples, banana chips, mangoes, dates, pineapples, figs, apricots, papayas, or raisins. Honey adds flavor to just about any breakfast food. For liquids, bring powdered juices and energy drinks.

Lunch: Bring bread that packs easily and won't be crushed, such as pita or bagels. Peanut butter and jelly packed in plastic squeeze bottles, cheese, and fresh vegetables are all good sandwich fillers. Dried fruit, nuts, seeds, granola, and chocolate are great for snacking, and energy bars and drinks help keep your legs moving.

A great way to save money and time is to pre-prepare your meals. Be sure to take foods that don't require refrigeration.

Dinner: Begin with a base of rice, pasta, or any quick-cooking grain. Pack fresh vegetables such as squash, onions, and carrots. Dried vegetables won't go bad, but they never taste as good either. Avoid meat, which can spoil, unless you are on a really short trip or you have a sag wagon and can keep it on ice. Remember, anything instant makes a good meal: potatoes, sauces, and soups are a few of the options.

Your body burns a lot of calories when you go on a bike tour. It is important to make sure you get enough to eat as you go. Otherwise, you may run out of energy and not be able to continue.

MAKE IT AHEAD

Another thing you may consider is how much riding you will do each day and how tired you might be at the end of a long day of biking. You may not have the energy to prepare a good meal. However, you can ensure that you have something ready to go by preparing your meals in advance. Pastas, chopped vegetables, and other simple ingredients can be prepped and put in bags so that all they need is reheating when you are done at the end of the day.

CHAPTER 4

SAFE TREKKING

Although you are not driving a car, following road safety rules is very important while bike trekking. Remember that you will sometimes be sharing the road with other cars and trucks, which can prove deadly in an encounter because you have less protection for your body. However, the following safety tips will keep you safer on the road.

FOLLOW ROAD RULES

Just as any bike rider would, it's safest to go with the flow of traffic by staying on the correct side of the road. If you are trekking in different countries, it's important to know what the flow of traffic is. You may actually need to switch sides depending on where you are. Staying with traffic reduces your chances of being hit. Also, always try to bike in a straight line. Never swerve into traffic and always

While some trekking takes place in remote areas, some will also happen on streets. Be aware of road rules to stay safe.

leave a little more than a car door's width of room between you and oncoming traffic as well as any parked vehicles.

Pay attention to lane markings. For example, don't go straight in a lane marked "left turn only." Obey traffic signs and signals. Not only is it dangerous to ride through stop signs and stoplights, it's also a quick way to cause an accident.

BE SEEN

Your bike should be well equipped with reflective surfaces and have a strong headlight and taillight mounted on the front and back.

Your bike should also include a bell and a rearview mirror. Reflectors on your wheels and panniers help drivers see you. You can also put reflective tape on other parts of your bike, your helmet, and on your clothing and shoes. Another good way to be seen is by wearing bright clothing. During the day, wear a bright windbreaker or jersey. Some riders like to attach a tall, reflective flag to one of their rear panniers to make it even easier for drivers to see them. If you are riding at night, wear something light-colored. At night, a reflector vest is also a must-have piece of safety gear.

Use hand signals anytime you need to make a move. By doing so, you are telling drivers where you are going and giving them

Bright colors on both clothing and equipment help other riders, drivers, and pedestrians see you coming.

time to avoid you. To signal a right-hand turn, either point straight out to the right with your right arm and hand, or bend your left arm at the elbow so that your left hand is straight up in the air. To signal a left-hand turn, just point straight out to the left with your left arm and hand. Remember in countries where drivers stay to the left, these rules are reversed. Straight out with your right hand indicates a right turn, and a bent right arm indicates a left turn. You should also signal to other riders in your group any time you are going to stop. You can do this by raising an arm straight up, with your palm out, and calling out ,"Stopping!"

If you come to a busy intersection and want to make a left-hand turn, you have a couple of choices: You can either turn like a car or cross the intersection like a pedestrian. To turn like a car, first look to your left for traffic, signal a left-hand turn, move into the left lane, then turn left with the flow of traffic. To cross the intersection like a pedestrian, get off your bike and walk it across the street in the crosswalk, then walk it across again to the left at the far crosswalk.

CAREFUL AND DEFENSIVE DRIVING

It is very important that any time you get on your bike you ride as if you are a target. This means you must always be on the defensive. Assume that no drivers can see you. Watch out for cars pulling out of driveways, switching lanes, swerving in front of you, and stopping suddenly. Try to make eye contact with a driver before you make any move to get in front of him or her.

It may sound like a lot of work paying attention to all the traffic in front of you and to your side, but it is even harder to watch the traffic behind you. Any time that you make a turn you must first look over your shoulder to make sure it is safe to do so. Move only when there are no vehicles in your way. This can be tricky. It is easy to lose your balance and swerve. Once you get the hang of it, though, the over-the-shoulder glance shouldn't be any problem at all.

Finally, do your best to avoid road hazards. This means constantly looking ahead for anything dangerous in the road such as glass, rocks, bottles and cans, ice, potholes, and sewage grates. Also be careful when crossing railroad tracks, speed bumps, and curbs. If you take them at the wrong angle, you run the risk of having your whole bike—gear and all—slide out from beneath you. Ride straight at them, at a right angle, and brace yourself as you go over them.

If you have to ride on a sidewalk or if your route takes you along a bike path shared by pedestrians, always give those on foot the right of way. If you are passing someone who is on foot, warn that person first by calling out. When crossing driveways or intersections, be particularly careful that no vehicles are about to pull out.

RIDING IN A GROUP

Group tours require that each member of the group take certain responsibilities so that everyone can act together as a team. Communication is very important during a group ride. If you are one in a line of cyclists, you have to work together. Warn the rider behind you when you are approaching an obstacle. If you see a rock, for instance, shout, "Rock!" This warning will give the cyclist behind you enough time to move to the side and avoid it.

Always ride single file. Keep several bike lengths' worth of space between you and the rider in front of you and behind you. It takes longer to come to a complete stop when your bike is weighted

Make sure that you have a pre-determined plan when you are bike trekking in a group, including emergency back-up plans.

PERFORMING SAFETY CHECKS

Using a checklist to ensure you and your bike are ready to go each time you head out is not just smart, it may also save you time.

Tires: Check to be sure they are properly inflated.

Brakes: Make sure they work. You can check the rear brake by squeezing the rear brake lever while pushing the bike forward. The rear wheel should skid. Check the front brake by doing the same thing with the front brake lever. The rear wheel should pop into the air. Make sure that the brake levers don't touch your handlebars when you squeeze them as tight as you can.

Quick releases: Check the releases on your seat and your front and rear wheels. Everything should be tight.

Lube: Lube up your chain and other moving parts. Well-lubed components are less likely to break.

Nuts and bolts: Check to make sure that nothing is loose or missing.

Helmet: Check for cracks. Make sure it fits correctly and all the straps are secure.

Wheels: Do they spin freely? Are they positioned correctly?

Other gear: Make sure you have everything. You don't want to start out on a long trip and then realize that you forgot to pack something important.

down with all your trekking gear—so keep this in mind when you are riding behind someone.

Develop a system of signals and warnings. For instance, shouting, "Car up!" warns the person behind you that a car is approaching in the opposite direction. "Car back!" warns all the riders ahead that a car will soon be passing them in the same lane and direction. When the person nearest you calls out a warning, make sure you pass that warning on to the next rider in line.

The world of bicycle trekking is still a relatively small one. Although millions of people ride bikes, few actually use their bikes to travel long distances. For the people who do trek, this is not a

When stopping for the night, make sure to store your bike properly to be sure that it is in good working condition for the next ride out.

problem—they prefer to have the roads to themselves. However, interest in this pastime is spreading and tour companies have joined in by sponsoring bike tours for travelers who want to see the world by riding through it. What's great about tours is that someone else deals with the logistics of the trip. They may even provide all of the equipment and give tourists a list of exactly what they need to bring along. These kinds of tours are great for people who are just starting out with bike trekking and need a little extra support. But veteran bike trekkers may find tours are too restrictive for their needs and the groups too large.

CHAPTER 5

WHAT'S NEW IN BIKE TREKKING

Bike trekking tours are quickly becoming big business. More and more people are looking for tours that support their ideals of staying fit and of leaving a smaller ecological footprint on the world, all while being able to see some incredible places up close. Bike trekking affords all of these things, and more. Tours may be local or international. Some support causes by raising money from the riders and sponsors. Some tours are very large and have planned-out itineraries, stops, and events, while other tours are smaller and can be more flexible.

Regardless of the type of tour that most interests you, all of them bring a sense of adventure to travel that may not be found in some other pursuits. The sport attracts adventurous spirits—those who prefer to take life by the reins and run rather than sit back and watch it go by. And more and more people are finding that spirit within themselves.

You won't be entirely alone if you decide to try bicycle trekking, but you will be different by the end. In a world of cars, planes, and high technology, pedal power is perceived as a throwback to the old days—a time when people had to use their legs to get where they wanted to go.

INCREDIBLE TRIPS

If you've got a mountain bike, some trekking experience, and an urge for serious adventure, you may want to consider bike trekking down an incredible route that takes three months to complete, like the Great Divide. Or maybe you want to bike trek for a cause. Then you might look into bike treks sponsored by the American Lung Association.

TREKKING THE GREAT DIVIDE

The mostly off-road Great Divide mountain bike route, established and mapped out by the Adventure Cycling Association, cuts a path from the Canada-Montana border over the steep passes of the southern Colorado Rockies and through the high desert of New Mexico. The route often climbs to elevations greater than 10,000 feet (3,000 meters).

Although there are many things Great Divide trekkers must do to prepare for this three-month cross-country trip, gaining an understanding of the mountains and how they will affect your trip is perhaps the most important. An extended tour at high altitudes—greater than 8,000 feet (2,400 meters) above sea level—can

Some organized bike trekking tours take you through beautiful landscapes, such as Moraine Lake in Banff National Park in Canada, pictured here.

be extremely challenging. At high altitudes, the body simply does not work the same way it does at lower elevations. Staying hydrated becomes extremely important. You have to change clothes almost as often as you change gears. And the weather can be perfect…or terrible.

The Great Divide route's creator, Michael McCoy, recommends riding the route from north to south and beginning in early July. By starting in the summer, you can avoid the heavy snow in the high mountains of the southern Colorado Rockies. And New Mexico—the high-desert part of the trip—can be biked in the fall, when the temperature is perfect for cycling.

Nevertheless, starting in July doesn't ensure that everything will go smoothly. The route commonly features three types of weather that can be dangerous for the unprepared rider. The first is rainstorms. You can expect rough conditions along many parts of the route if it gets wet.

"It can get real slick and impassable when you get into rainy periods," says McCoy. "The mud cakes up so badly in your tires that you can't go anywhere." But there is a solution: "Always carry a day or two of extra food in case you have to hole up for a while," McCoy says.

The second weather danger is cold. Cold rain, wind, and snow can occur at any time, even in the summer. "It might be 90 degrees [32 degrees Celsius] when you set out from some valley town in Colorado," says McCoy, "but on the same day you can run into dangerously cold weather conditions up high." To avoid serious

Be prepared for variable temperatures, including extreme hot and cold, as well as rough terrain and weather changes.

problems, pack your panniers with warm clothing and lots of food and water.

Finally, trekkers need to beware of lightning. Dark thunderclouds are very common on summer afternoons at a high altitude. "You might be caught in a thunderstorm while two miles away the sun is still shining," says McCoy. If you're caught in a storm, stay away from tall trees and crouch close to the ground in a low area. Try sitting on your panniers, keeping your body, especially your feet, off the ground.

TREKKING FOR A CAUSE

If you're interested in trekking for a good cause, the American Lung Association could use your help. The ALA, a national organization that works to combat lung diseases such as asthma, emphysema, and cancer, sponsors many health programs, fundraisers, and special events around the country. One of these events is the annual Big Ride Across America.

Members of the Big Ride team in Washington, DC, in 2014.

The Big Ride is a 48-day, 3,250-mile (5,230-kilometer), fully supported bicycle trek from Seattle, Washington,

LEAVE NO TRACE

The national Leave No Trace organization has outlined some simple rules you can use to keep the environment healthy. Bicycle tourists need to think about their impact to the environment. Don't litter, ride off the road or trail, or camp in fragile natural areas. These can hurt the land and the animals that you are riding through. The following six principles will help you to do your part for the environment while enjoying your bike trek:

1. Plan ahead and prepare. Know where you're going, how to get there, and what you will need to make the trip.
2. Travel and camp on durable surfaces. Don't ride or camp on anything that can't handle your bike or tent.
3. Leave nothing behind. Pack out everything you pack in, including food scraps, trash, and toilet paper. If you can't find a trash can, pack it away and hold on to it until later.
4. Properly dispose of what you can't pack out. This means always carry out or bury your waste!
5. Leave what you find the same way that you found it. Everything has its place and its purpose. Leave things for others to enjoy.
6. Minimize the use and impact of fire. If you have to make a campfire, be careful not to leave any sign of it once it is out.

to Washington, DC As participants pedal across America's heartland, they raise money and awareness for the ALA's fight against lung disease.

SAFE TREKKING TIPS

Whether you are trekking an incredible route like the Great Divide or not, you need to be aware of the basic things you need to make it through. Look back at the checklists in this resource and be sure to plan out your route and your stops if you are going on your own or with a small group. Here are some other tips.

EXPECT THE UNEXPECTED

Be prepared for whatever the route will throw your way, including sudden cold or heat, rain, hail, snow, sleet, fog, lightning, high winds, or glare. Remember that at very high elevations, regardless of where you are on the globe, it can be very hot during the day and freezing at night. Storms can come in fast. If you see scary-looking clouds, find shelter immediately. Don't wait until the storm rolls on you. Fill your panniers with essentials like warm fleece, windproof and waterproof outer gear, pants, hats, gloves, extra food, and water.

KNOW YOUR FIRST AID

You may be far from help when things go wrong. Know what to do in an emergency. Carry a first-aid kit and learn CPR (cardiopulmonary resuscitation) and basic first aid before you leave home.

PAY ATTENTION TO YOUR BODY

It can be difficult to breathe at high altitudes. Your body needs oxygen, and the air is thinner the higher up you go, which means you could become oxygen-deprived very quickly. Give your body time to acclimatize. Stop often and give your body a chance to get used to the thin air. While it does, you can rest. Once you get acclimatized, you can get started again and you will find that it's easier to ride.

If you begin to feel ill, stop. Let the other people in your group know as soon as possible so that you can get care if needed.

You also need to pay attention to your body's need for water and food. Drink as much water as you can. As you exercise, you will lose water through sweat so it's important to have water close at hand to replenish what you have lost. When your body is dehydrated it does not work as efficiently. You might even black out. Your body also burns calories while riding, so be sure to replace those calories with food along the way.

GLOSSARY

ASTHMA A condition that is characterized by wheezing and difficulty breathing, and often accompanied by coughing and constriction in the chest.

BRAIN BUCKET The inside part of a helmet that cradles the head.

DRAFT Riding in a line to reduce wind resistance.

EMPHYSEMA A lung disease in which the lung tissue has been destroyed and there is abnormal enlargement of air spaces in the lungs.

FENDER A piece of metal or plastic mounted over the wheels of a bicycle to reduce splashing from mud or water.

GEAR Tools that are used for a particular occupation or activity.

HOSTEL A supervised lodging place for young people.

IODINE An element often used in medicine as an antiseptic.

PACE A steady speed.

PANNIER A basket or bag that is used for carrying provisions that is attached over a bicycle's rear wheel.

POLYPROPYLENE A plastic polymer used for insulation.

REMOTE Secluded or out of the way.

SWERVE An abrupt turn from a straight course.

TERRAIN The physical features of a piece of land or road.

WICK To draw liquid away from something.

FOR MORE INFORMATION

Adventure Cycling Association
150 East Pine Street
PO Box 8308
Missoula, MT 59807
(800) 755-2453
Website: http://www.adventurecycling.org
Established in 1973, this nonprofit organization aims to inspire and empower people to travel by bicycle. It has 48,000 members in North America and has routes, maps, and guided tours for bike enthusiasts.

Alliance for Biking & Walking
PO Box 65150
Washington, DC 20035
(202) 449-9692
Website: http://www.bikewalkalliance.org
The goal of this nonprofit organization is to support local advocacy organizations in order to create walk- and bicycle-friendly communities.

Bicycle Adventure Club
PO Box 23998
San Diego, CA 92193
(858) 715-9510
office@bicycleadventureclub.org
Website: http://www.bicycleadventureclub.org
This nonprofit bicycle touring club is run by 1,500 volunteer members who create bicycle tours in the United States and internationally. Membership is open to cyclists eighteen years of age and older.

Canadian Cycling Association
2197 Riverside Drive, Suite 203
Ottawa, ON K1H 7X3
Canada
(613) 248-1353

general@cyclingcanada.ca
Website: http://www.cyclingcanada.ca
This government-funded group is responsible for promoting all types of cycling as well as overseeing bicycling teams and organizing competitions.

Charity Treks
PO Box 321
Charlottesville, VA 22902
Website: http://www.charitytreks.org
This volunteer-run nonprofit organization brings riders and volunteers from across the United States and Canada to participate in charity rides to benefit AIDS research with the goal of helping to fund a vaccine.

League of American Bicyclists
1612 K Street NW, Suite 308
Washington, DC 20006
(202) 822-1333
Website: http://www.bikeleague.org
This league was founded in 1880 by "wheelmen" who were challenged by rutted roads of gravel and dirt and wanted to improve riding conditions. The organization's mission is to facilitate the enjoyment of cycling by ensuring that the Unites States is bicycle-friendly for all.

People for Bikes
PO Box 2359
Boulder, CO 80306
(303) 449-4893
info@peopleforbikes.org
Website: http://www.peopleforbikes.org
This group unites all people who are involved in biking and cycling, from casual riders to commuters, bike trekkers, and bike shop owners, in an effort to provide a unified front in advocacy for cyclists at the local and national level.

WEBSITES

Because of the changing nature of Internet links, Rosen Publishing has developed an online list of websites related to the subject of this book. This site is updated regularly. Please use this link to access the list:

http://www.rosenlinks.com/OUT/Bike

FOR FURTHER READING

Allwood, Mel. *The Total Bike Maintenance Book: DIY Repairs Made Easy*. London, England: Carlton Books, 2012.

Andrews, Guy. *Bike Mechanic: Tales from the Road and the Workshop*. Boulder, CO: Velo Press, 2014.

Bridge, Raymond. *Bike Touring: The Sierra Club Guide to Travel on Two Wheels*. San Francisco, CA: Sierra Club Books, 2009.

Burke, Edmund R., and Ed Pavelka. *The Complete Book of Long-Distance Cycling: Build the Strength, Skills, and Confidence to Ride as Far as You Want*. New York, NY: Rodale Books, 2000.

Embacher, Michael. *Cyclepedia: A Century of Iconic Bicycle Design*. San Francisco, CA: Chronicle Books, 2011.

Hallett, Richard. *The Bike Deconstructed: A Grand Tour of the Modern Bicycle*. Princeton, NJ: Princeton Architectural Press, 2014.

Lord, Stephen. *Adventure Cycle-Touring Handbook: Worldwide Cycling Route & Planning Guide*. Hindhead, England: Trailblazer Publications, 2010.

Santella, Chris. *Fifty Places to Bike Before You Die: Biking Experts Share the World's Greatest Destinations*. New York, NY: Stewart, Tabori & Chang, 2012.

Stutzman, Paul. *Biking Across America: My Coast-to-Coast Adventure and the People I Met Along the Way*. Grand Rapids, MI: Revell, 2013.

Zinn, Lennard. *Zill & the Art of Road Bike Maintenance: The World's Best-Selling Bicycle Repair and Maintenance Guide*. Boulder, CO: Velo Press, 2013.

INDEX

ABOUT THE AUTHORS

Melody Wayne writes and edits from her home in Brooklyn, New York. She is an amateur cyclist looking forward to her first bike trekking trip.

Chris Hayhurst has written more than thirty books for middle and high school students. He has received awards from the American Association of Educational Publishers and the American Library Association.

PHOTO CREDITS

Cover, p. 1, dolomite-summits/Shutterstock.com; pp. 4-5 © Jon Sparks/Alamy; pp. 8-9 moodboard/Thinkstock; p. 10 Cultura/Gandalf Hammerbacher/Getty Images; p. 13 Oksana Perkins/iStock/Thinkstock; pp. 14-15 Mike Watson Images/moodboard/Thinkstock; pp. 18-19 bodu9/iStock/Thinkstock; p. 21 Rich Wheater/All Canada Photos/Getty Images; p. 24 © al churcher/Alamy; p. 26 Jordan Siemens/Iconica/Getty Images; p. 29 wavebreakmedia/Shutterstock.com; p. 33 Zerbor/Shutterstock.com; p. 35 Daxiao Productions/Shutterstock.com; p. 36 Monkik/Shutterstock.com; p. 38 Dejan Dundjerski/Shutterstock.com; p. 41 connel/Shutterstock.com; p. 42 Tyler Olson/Shutterstock.com; pp. 44-45 Henn Photography/Cultura/Getty Images; p. 47 Jupiterimages/Pbotos.com/Thinkstock; p. 51 All Rights By Krishna. Wu/Moment/Getty Images; p. 52 Alexander Fortelny/E+/Getty Images; p. 53 Pedego Electric Bikes/AP Images; p. 56 Purestock/Getty Images; cover and interior pages Iwona Grodzka/iStock/Thinkstock (twig frame), AKIRA/amanaimagesRF/Thinkstock (wood frame)

Designer: Brian Garvey; Editor: Tracey Baptiste

Photo researcher: Karen Huang